A Note to Parents and Teachers

DK READERS is a compelling program for beginning readers, designed in conjunction with leading literacy experts.

Beautiful illustrations and superb full-color photographs combine with engaging, easy-to-read stories to offer a fresh approach to each subject in the series. Each DK READER is guaranteed to capture a child's interest while developing his or her reading skills, general knowledge, and love of reading.

The five levels of DK READERS are aimed at different reading abilities, enabling you to choose the books that are exactly right for your child:

Pre-level 1 – Learning to read
Level 1 – Beginning to read
Level 2 – Beginning to read alone
Level 3 – Reading alone
Level 4 – Proficient readers

The "normal" age at which a child begins to read can be anywhere from three to eight years old, so these levels are only a general guideline.

No matter which level you select, you can be sure that you are helping your child learn to read, then read to learn!

LONDON, NEW YORK, MUNICH,
MELBOURNE, AND DELHI

Editor Kate Simkins
Senior Art Editor Nick Avery
Art Director Mark Richards
Publishing Manager Simon Beecroft
Category Publisher Alex Kirkham
Production Rochelle Talary
DTP Designer Lauren Egan

For Lucasfilm
Art Editor Iain R. Morris
Senior Editor Jonathan W. Rinzler
Continuity Supervisor Leland Chee

Reading Consultant
Linda B. Gambrell, Professor and
Director, Eugene T. Moore School of
Education, Clemson University.

First American Edition, 2005
Published in the United States by
DK Publishing, Inc.
375 Hudson Street
New York, New York 10014

10 11 12 10 9 8 7

Published in Great Britain by Dorling Kindersley Limited.

A catalog record for this book is available from
the Library of Congress

ISBN-13: 978-0-7566-1146-0 (hb)
ISBN-13: 978-0-7566-1157-6 (pb)

Color reproduction by Media Development and Printing, UK
Printed and bound in China by L. Rex Printing Co. Ltd.

Discover more at
www.dk.com
www.starwars.com

DK READERS

LUCAS BOOKS

STAR WARS™
What is a
Wookiee?

Written by Laura Buller and Kate Simkins

BEGINNING
1
TO READ

My name
is C-3PO.

I am a droid.
I am a talking
machine.

I live far, far away in space.
Lots of creatures live here.
I will be telling you
about some of them.

Space

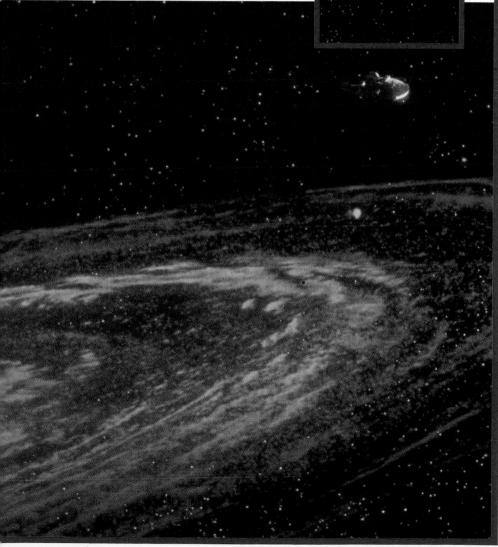

5

Some creatures in *Star Wars* are aliens.

Aliens are not human.
There are lots of different aliens.

Humans also live here—
my friend Padmé (PAD-MAY) is
a human.

This is my friend R2-D2.
He is a droid too.

R2-D2 likes talking.
His voice sounds like
whistles and beeps, but
I can understand him.

R2-D2 is a clever
little machine.
He has all sorts
of useful tools.
He can fix anything!

Tool

Meet Chewbacca.

He is a tall,
furry alien
called
a Wookiee.

He is the best friend of Han Solo, who is a human.
They fly a spaceship together.

Sometimes,
I ride with them!

Spaceship

Now say hello
to Jar Jar Binks.

He is a friendly
alien.

Jar Jar comes from
an underwater city.
On land, Jar Jar is always
falling over!

He uses his long tongue
to catch food to eat.

Let's visit Watto's shop.

Watto is a blue alien.
He has a bad temper.
Watto flies about
using the wings on his back.

He sells bits of old machines
called junk.

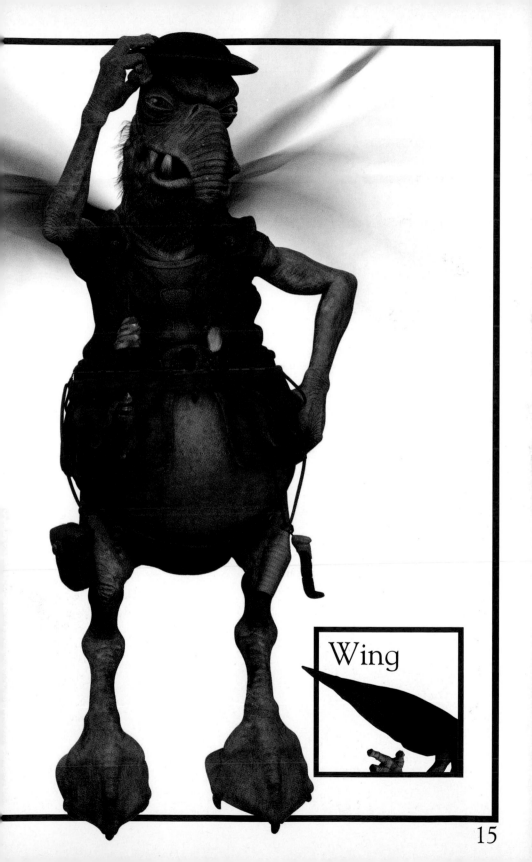

Wing

Now it's time
to meet Sebulba
(SEE-BUL-BAH).

This nasty alien races in a vehicle called a Podracer. He likes to go fast.

Podracer

Sebulba will do anything to win. He will even throw things at other Podracers!

Pit droids fix the Podracers.
They are very useful and
can carry heavy things.

Pit droids sometimes
get into trouble.
There is one way to stop them.
Tap them on the nose
and they fold up.

Jabba the Hutt is a nasty alien.
He has a fat body and a long tail.
His body is covered in sticky slime.

Tail

Jabba's eyes are red and yellow
and his breath is smelly.
Don't get too near him!

Let's visit Dexter Jettster's restaurant.

This friendly alien has four arms. He cooks the food at Dexter's Diner.

Dexter knows lots of things.
What shall we ask him?

These creatures
are lizard keepers.

They live
in big holes
in the ground.

Sometimes, the lizard keepers ride around on giant lizards. The lizards are good at jumping and climbing.

Jawas are small creatures
with shiny yellow eyes.

Their faces
are hidden under
the hoods of
their brown cloaks.

Hood

These little aliens
find droids and
bits of machines to sell.

Once, they even sold
R2-D2!

If we go deep into the forest,
we may meet the Ewoks.

Ewoks are small, furry creatures.
They live in houses
that they build high up
in the trees.

Forest

Yoda is very old and very wise.
He has green skin and
big, pointy ears.

No one knows what kind
of creature he is or
where he comes from.

I hope you have enjoyed
learning about the creatures
in *Star Wars*.

Goodbye!

Picture word list

Space

page 5

Podracer

page 17

Tool

page 9

Tail

page 20

Spaceship

page 11

Hood

page 26

Wing

page 15

Forest

page 29